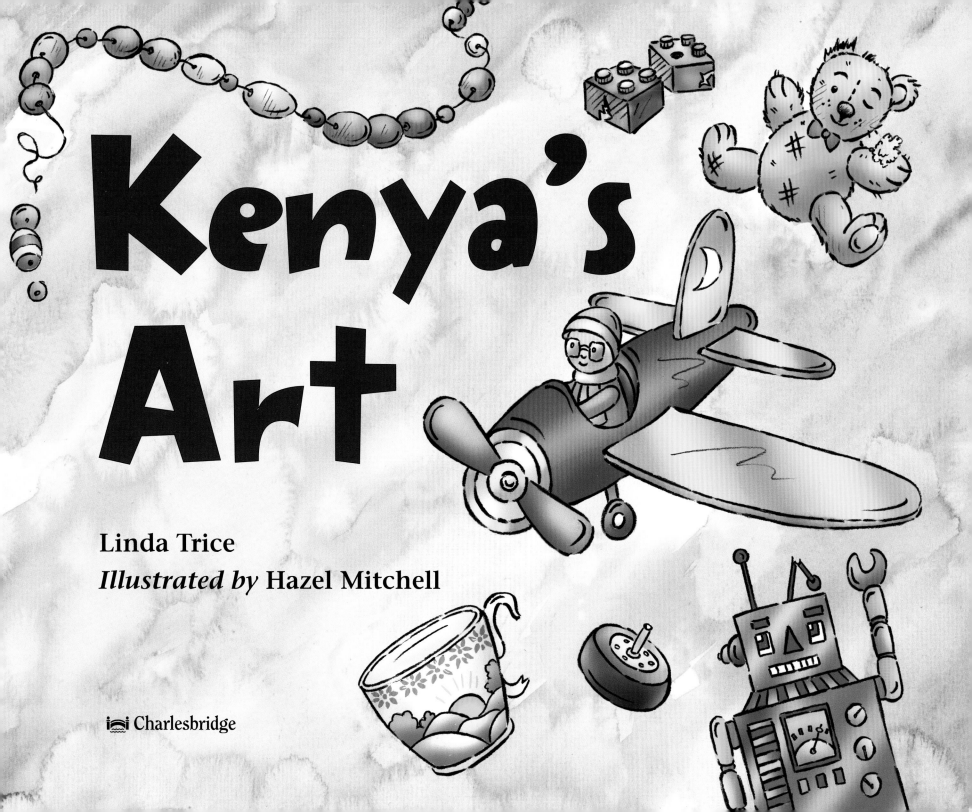

Kenya's Art

Linda Trice

Illustrated by Hazel Mitchell

ini Charlesbridge

To the Simmons sisters: Bryce, Genevieve, and Rhys—L. T.

To those who inspire with art, everywhere—H. M.

Thank you to the people whose advice and support made this book possible: Kent Brown, executive director, Highlights Foundation; Myrna Harrison-Changar, detritus artist; Professor David Driskell, artist and African American art scholar; and Yolanda Scott, editorial director, Charlesbridge.—Linda Trice

Published by Charlesbridge
85 Main Street
Watertown, MA 02472
(617) 926-0329
www.charlesbridge.com

Library of Congress Cataloging-in-Publication Data
Trice, Linda, author.
  Kenya's art / Linda Trice.
    pages cm
  Summary: Instructed to get rid of all her broken toys, Kenya, with the help of her father, recycles them into art for her class project.
  ISBN 978-1-57091-848-3 (reinforced for library use)
  ISBN 978-1-60734-834-4 (ebook)
  ISBN 978-1-60734-835-1 (ebook pdf)
  1. Mobiles (Sculpture)—Juvenile fiction. 2. Found objects (Art)—Juvenile fiction.
3.Creative ability—Juvenile fiction. 4. African American families—Juvenile fiction.
[1. Recycling (Waste)—Fiction. 2. Art—Fiction. 3. African Americans—Fiction. 4.
Family life—Fiction.] I. Title.
PZ7.T73355Kb 2016
[E]—dc23   2014049634

Printed in China
(hc) 10 9 8 7 6 5 4 3 2 1

Illustrations created with watercolor and graphite and over-painted digitally
Display type and text type set in Stone Serif designed by Sumner Stone for Linotype
Color separations by Colourscan Print Company Pte Ltd, Singapore
Printed by C & C Offset Printing Co. Ltd. in Shenzhen, Guangdong, China
Production supervision by Brian G. Walker
Designed by Susan Mallory Sherman

"**W**hy are you playing with that old airplane?" Mosi asked.
"It's my prize," Kenya said. "I won it in art class."
"That was two years ago," Mosi said.

"Kenya, I asked you to get rid of your broken toys," Mom said.
"But I won this airplane, Mom," Kenya replied. "The art teacher said my drawing was the most original."

"It only has one wing," Mom said. "Get rid of all your broken toys, even that airplane. Then ask Daddy to help you with your school project. I'm taking Mosi to her friend's party."

"Daddy, I need help with my homework," Kenya said.

"What do you have to do?" he asked.

"I have to tell the class what I did during spring vacation," Kenya said. "I haven't done anything."

"It's time to take the towels out of the dryer," Daddy said. "I can teach you how to fold them."

"That's not fun," Kenya said.

"You could learn how to match the clean socks," Daddy said with a smile.

"Daddy, you're silly," Kenya said. "Let's go to the park," Daddy said. "Maybe we'll find something there."

On the way to the park, Daddy and Kenya saw the twins, Genevieve and Bryce, with their new puppy.

"Sit, Jack," Bryce said. He did.

"We taught him that during spring vacation," Genevieve said.

"Wow!" Kenya said.
"What did you do, Kenya?" Genevieve asked.
"Nothing," Kenya said.

Daddy and Kenya sat on a park bench.
"What is that loud noise?" Kenya asked.

Noah marched up to them, blowing his trumpet. "I took music lessons during spring vacation," he said. "What did you do, Kenya?"

"Nothing," Kenya said.

"I won a prize at soccer camp," Marie said as she kicked her ball. "What did you do, Kenya?"

"Nothing," Kenya said.

"I want to go to vacation camp," Kenya told Daddy.

"They are over by now," he said.

"Can I get a kitten?" Kenya asked. "I could teach it how to sit and fetch. I could win a prize."

"You are not getting a kitten," Daddy said, laughing.

"But I need something to show in class on Monday," Kenya said.

"We'll take a tour at the museum," Daddy said. "You can tell your class what you learn."

Ms. Alvarez showed them some plastic water bottles that were glued together with colorful streamers around them.

"This artist recycled used bottles and made something to look at. It's not useful, it's art."

"That's a thingamabob!" Kenya whispered to Daddy. "My art teacher said a thingamabob is something creative that doesn't have another name."

"You don't have to throw everything away," Ms. Alvarez said. "Is it clean? Is it safe to use? Can you make something useful from it, or make it into art? Recycle! Reuse! Make art!"

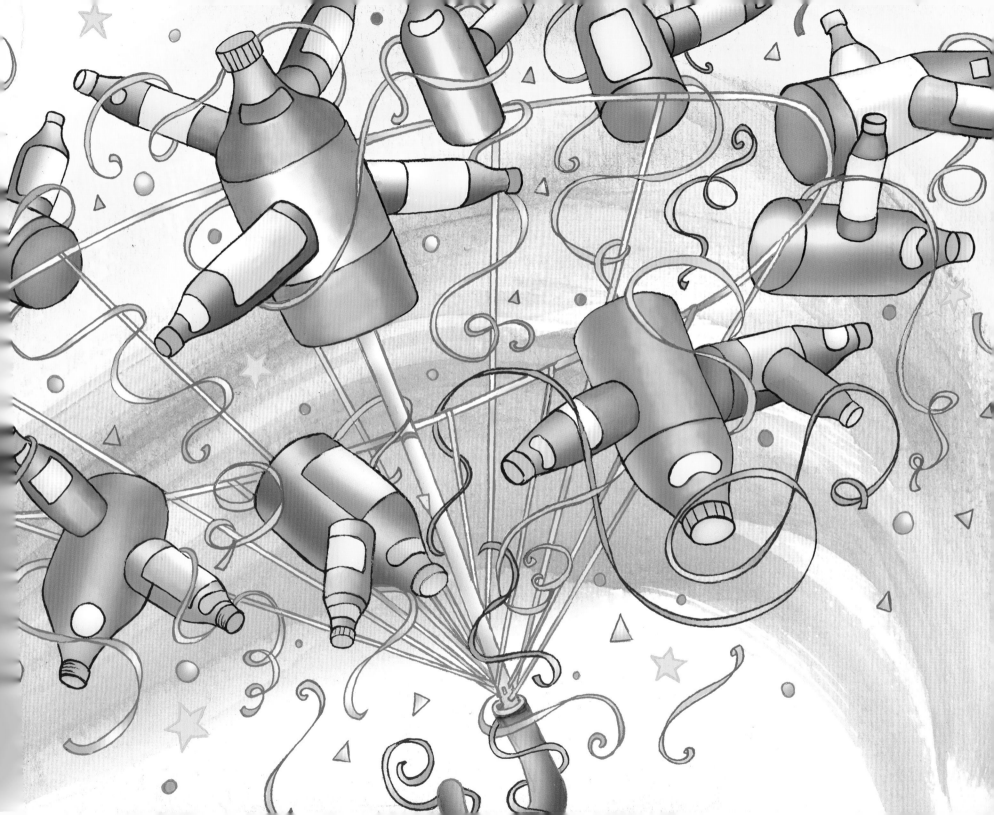

RECYCLE! REUSE!

"Recycle! Reuse! Make art!" Kenya and Daddy chanted as they walked home.

Suddenly Kenya knew what she could do for her spring vacation project. She told Daddy her idea.

"That's great," he said. "The whole family can do it together."

"The museum guide told us we can use recycled items to make useful things or fun art," Kenya told Mom and Mosi.

"Let's all 'Recycle! Reuse! Make art!'" Daddy said.

Kenya found toys that she didn't play with anymore. She brought them into the kitchen. "They're all clean and safe to use," she said. A toy truck had only one wheel. A doll had no hair.

"Nobody would want those toys," Mom said.

"Recycle! Reuse! Make art!" Kenya and Daddy sang as the family worked.
Mom found an old picture frame. She painted it and glued beads from a
broken necklace around the edges. "I made something useful," Mom said.
Kenya touched the pretty frame and said, "I can hardly see the scratches."

"I cut out pictures from an old magazine and glued them on construction paper," Mosi said.

"It's a card for your friend!" Mom said.

"You made something useful, Mosi," Daddy said.

Daddy made a face on a paper plate. He glued on buttons for eyes, a paper flower for a nose, and a broken barrette for a mouth. He added one of his old ties. "It's me," he said. "I made art."

"It doesn't look anything like you," Kenya said. "Daddy, you're silly!"

Kenya stuck broken toys into colored clay. She added the airplane with the missing wing. Then she tied everything together with string and hair ribbons. "I made art, too," she said.

"It's original," Mom said as she looked at it.

"It's creative," Daddy said.

"I made a thingamabob," Kenya said. "It's something that has no other name."

"You got rid of your broken toys, too," Mom said. "Good job, Kenya."

"You can tell your class that you learned to 'Recycle! Reuse! Make art!' during your spring vacation," Daddy said.

"How was everyone's vacation?" Mrs. Garcia asked the class on Monday.

"I read three books," Ava said.

"I'm so proud of you," Mrs. Garcia said.

"I went to Florida and picked oranges in my grandma's backyard," Debbie said.
"Thanks!" everyone said as she shared the oranges.

"I milked a cow all by myself," Josh said.

"Wow!" everyone said.

Kenya didn't say anything. She just smiled.

"What did you do, Kenya?" Mrs. Garcia asked.

"I learned to 'Recycle! Reuse! Make art!' at the museum," Kenya said.

"Did you make anything, Kenya?" Mrs. Garcia asked.

"I made a thingamabob!" Kenya said. "I can show everyone how to make one!"